THE GIRL WITH THE SHOULDS

Written and Illustrated By Barbara Van Kirk

Cover Design By Kerrie Tatone

ISBN 0-9631751-1-4

The New Beginning

Published by The New Beginning
1340 North Juniper
Canby, Oregon 97013
2nd Printing 1993

FOR MYSELF AND ALL MY SISTERS...

With special thanks to Ross and Janice,
and Dan and Nan (for telling me I could do it),
Sam and Alice (for their support and suggestions),
my husband Larry (who did the dishes),
Mickey Tate (who offered good advice),
Caroline Lake (who reminded me of my self confidence),
and Mary Helen Smith (who helps me find it from time to time...).

I once sat down to ponder
Just who was controlling my life
I found many things to consider
As the cause of all of my strife

Doctors had control of my body
My boss told me what I should do
Preachers and teachers were filling my mind
And my neighbor had shoulds for me to

Traveling folks said I should see the world
My family said I should stay near
A motherly lady said I should make a home
My friends said I should have a career

I took their shoulds every chance that I could
And I tried to apply them to me
But I got weighted down with the shoulds that I found
'Til finally I was no longer free

Once there was a very little girl.

Her family gave her
many things to help
her grow up.
They gave her <u>affection,</u>
so she could share
it with others.

3

They gave her
<u>self-confidence,</u>
so she could try
new things.

And they gave her
<u>shoulds,</u>
so she would be
safe and happy.

7

9

And, her family gave
her two special shoulds
that had been passed
down through generations.

And she took them.

When she was older
she got some shoulds
from outside the family.

The Sunday school teacher
had some for her.

And
the neighbor lady
had some too.

Even strangers
offered her shoulds...
and she took them all.

19

Where ever she went
she carried her affection
and her self-confidence
and all her shoulds with her.

The girl grew older
and went to school.
There the teachers
gave her many shoulds.
And so did her friends.

23

The girl became a
young lady.
She was very happy.

Then ...
one day someone
presented her with
a big, heavy should.

27

It said:

She took it.

Another time a
person offered her
a should that was
even heavier.

It said:

And
she took it.

On another day
someone delivered
her a should that
was the heaviest
of all.

35

It said:

YOU
SHOULD
PUT ALL
OTHERS
FIRST

(It looked like
it weighed
a ton)

But - she took it.

By now the girl
had become a
dedicated collector
of shoulds.

She had one that said:

One that said:

YOU
SHOULD
NEVER
GET
ANGRY

One that said:

One that said:

and,
one that said:

She had one that said:

YOU *SHOULD* ALWAYS LOOK PERFECT

And one that said:

Eventually,
her house was
filled with shoulds

and they had gotten
too heavy to carry around.

One evening, the girl decided to go out and enjoy herself.

She dressed <u>perfectly.</u>
She practiced <u>being nice.</u>
She made <u>no mistakes.</u>

49

But then she realized
she could not go out.

Her shoulds were
too heavy to carry,
and she had lost her
self-confidence.
(It had been
buried with shoulds!)

She was very sad.

53

Luckily, the girl had
a friend who was familiar
with shoulds and what a
heavy burden they can
be. The girl called her
friend and the friend
came right over.

The girl said, "I have tried to please everyone else... and now I'm weighted down with shoulds that others have given me. I can't be myself anymore and my self-confidence is gone."

57

And the friend said, "We need to break the shoulds your family passed down through generations. You don't need to always please others and be everything nice."

So, they broke those
shoulds into pieces.

The friend helped the girl sort through all the shoulds. It was hard work because she had to decide which ones she wanted to keep ...

and which
ones were
too heavy
to carry.

61

It took a long time.

But finally
they had checked
them all.

And when they were
finished they found
the girl's self-confidence!

65

Now ...
the girl tries to
be responsible for
choosing only those
shoulds she can handle.

(She doesn't accept
every should that
is offered to her.)

Today, the girl still carries
her shoulds with her.
She carries them along with
her self-confidence ...

and the affection
she shares with others.

73

75

ORDER INFORMATION FOR
BOOKS FROM THE NEW BEGINNING
BY BARBARA VAN KIRK

"The Person Who Had Feelings": Read about a person who wore his feelings
on his sleeves. A story of loneliness, fear and anger; of sharing and
friendship and acceptance.

"The Girl With The Shoulds" and "The Person Who Had Feelings"
can be purchased by mail for $8.95 per copy, plus $2.50 shipping.
Please include your check with your order
(add $.75 in shipping costs for each additional book)
and send to :
THE NEW BEGINNING
1340 N. Juniper, Canby, Oregon 97013